I0692133

Hungry Foxes
on Our Hillside

BARBARA HATTEMER

Illustrated by Amber Waters

Copyright © 2017 Barbara Hattemer
All rights reserved.
ISBN: 978-1-945975-16-5

Published by EA Books Publishing a division of
Living Parables of Central Florida, Inc. a 501c3
EABooksPublishing.com

DEDICATION

Dedicated to my beloved Grandchildren

Mikayla and Caeden Cooley,

who pick blueberries and play with me on our

favorite hillside in Maine,

the hillside the foxes visited all summer!

Hello, my name is Mikayla, Caeden is my brother.

We love to visit our beloved grandmother.

All summer she lives on an island in Maine;
Her house sits in the woods on a small dirt lane.

One summer she helped us plant red maple trees
Then they were seedlings but now have more leaves.
Deep red they stand out, their branches are full
Grandma's favorite hillside is incredibly cool!

Her hill is strong granite that rises up high
On top, tall spruce trees reach toward the sky.
It's full of needles, mosses, and many ground covers
A delight for rock cranberry and blueberry lovers.

We watch it with Grandma, hear its sounds, see each sight
And wonder what animals play there at night.
We have watched mother deer with their fawns bounding by.
Bald eagles, red-headed woodpeckers swoop down from the sky.

Last year minks entertained us, a family of five,

Her beautiful hillside is so often alive

With an array of God's creatures who stop by for a while

To warm our hearts and make us all smile.

This summer on her hillside what did we see

But two little foxes prancing with glee

Dragging a seagull, its wingspread was long

Its belly was round, its wings must have been strong.

How did little foxes take a gull from the sky?

Or did it fall on her hillside, we wondered why.

Did God provide them this incredible meal?

Is what we are seeing actually real?

We asked our Grandma why the gull had been killed.

Were clumsy little foxes really that skilled?

Could they land a gull and perform such strife?
She explained it was simply the cycle of life.
For foxes to live, they must eat to survive;
God provides for them food that is often alive.
He has given them skills to hunt for their prey
It will keep them alive wherever they stay.

Sometimes they find food that is already dead
It helps His wild animals that need to be fed.
He provides what they need one way or the other
We both were comforted by our dear grandmother.

One climbed onto the stump, disappeared in its hollow,
Then resurfaced again. The hole must have been shallow.

They dashed across the hillside before starting their meal
Looking for anything that would enhance its appeal.

For salad, one fox found my red maple tree
And plucked with his teeth a succulent leaf.
He foraged for grubs all over the ground
For dessert he ate blueberries that were juicy and round.

For a full thirty minutes they ate and they played;

What a wonder of nature before us was laid!

Thank you, Lord, for this beautiful world you created

We delight in your animals, 'specially those who have mated.

The next day they returned to their prey with their mother;

We waited to see if they might have a brother.

Mother fox stood up high overlooking their play

We wondered if she would allow them to stay.

She posed on our hilltop, then walked all across
The beautiful gray green reindeer moss.
As black clouds rolled in and thunder peals roared
The foxes disappeared and all the birds soared.

From inside Caeden and I watched rain start to fall

Soon it pelted our hillside, wind bending trees large and small.

Not a single animal anywhere could be seen

And the roar of nature became incredibly mean.

Then a thunderous crack splintered a tall spruce tree
It uprooted a clump and brought down all three.
Our hillside was covered with branches high in the air,
The foxes must have had a terrible scare.

Would they return to our hill or would they stay away
Remembering the danger of that frightful day?
Grandma had the trees removed as soon as she could
And we waited and watched the edge of the woods.

Three days later the kits bounded onto the hill
As playful as ever, we were all thrilled.
All summer long a fox returned now and then;
Somewhere nearby must be the site of their den.

The last time we saw them was the best time of all
When they entered the stump and shot out like a ball.
They dashed round to the back and jumped in again
Just like Caeden and I play on our jungle gym.

The day came when mother fox felt they were grown
And led them to territory that would soon be their own.

Wherever you are, dear foxes, may your life be good
And may you do all the things that young foxes should.

With your nose to the ground, poke through the moss.

Search and find, then, with a sudden toss,

Conquer a vole, a favorite fox food.

May that put you both in a very good mood.

May you grow and prosper and find a mate;

I hope a new family will be your fate.

May we return to see you all playing here

As you did all summer this special year!

LEARN MORE ABOUT RED FOXES

RED FOXES are brown at birth, have a red coat when they are one month old, and some red foxes have a beautiful golden, reddish brown coat as adults. They have thick furry tails with a white tip which they use to keep their balance, to keep warm in winter, and to communicate with other foxes. They often have black ears and legs.

They are good parents, very playful, friendly, curious, intelligent, cunning and resourceful.

A baby fox is called a kit or a cub.

They hunt for food all the time and eat most anything: berries, vegetables, rodents, rabbits, wild birds, fish, spiders, poultry, reptiles, insects, frogs, worms, eggs.

Rodents like mice and voles are their favorite foods. Their hearing is so good, they can pounce on a small animal under the ground, locating it by sound. In the snow, they listen and pounce head down at whatever they hear crawling underground. 75% of the time, they find a meal.

They have small tummies so they eat many small meals a day. If they find food and aren't hungry, they save it for another day.

Sometimes, when they are not hungry, they will play with a mouse until they get bored, then let him go.

They belong to the dog, wolf and coyote families, but they have many qualities of a cat. Large triangular ears help them hear rodents scurrying about under the ground. They have whiskers on their legs and narrow faces that help them find their way. They walk on their toes like a cat with an elegant gait. They can climb trees and are very active at night. And they can run 30 miles an hour.

They are found all around the world in forests, grasslands, mountains, and deserts especially in the Northern Hemisphere. They live in underground dens where they take care of their kits and hide from larger animals who would hurt them.

Babies are born in the winter. Their parents take care of them all through the summer. In the fall they strike out on their own.

A vixen (a female fox) can have from 1 to 12 kits. They can live up to 14 years, but only 3 or 4 years in the wild.

Red foxes can scream, bark, howl and whine. They can communicate with each other with 28 calls and can make up to 40 sounds.

When raised with humans from birth, they can make very good and loving pets.

References

1. Foxes: Facts and Pictures by Alina Bradford, Live Science Contributor, May 23, 2014

2. What Do Foxes Eat/What Do Red Foxes Eat—Animals Time by Waleed Khalid

3. 2015 WolfPark.org

4. Nwf.org/wildlife-library/Mammals/Red-Fox.aspx – National Wildlife Federation

5. Answers.yahoo.com -- What do red foxes eat?

ABOUT THE AUTHOR

Barbara attended Smith College and Harvard Business School and worked for a Management Consulting firm before marrying and raising four children. She now has eight grandchildren and four great grandchildren.

To bless friends and relatives, she began writing rhyming poetry when she was a child and has recently returned to it. *Hungry Foxes on Our Hillside* reflects her love for nature and God's provision for the animals he has created. It is her first Children's Book.

Over many years Barbara has been published in a wide variety of magazines. Her first full length book *The Impact of the Media on Children and the Family*, detailed the harms of sexually explicit and violent media.

She now writes novels about difficult subjects that she makes fun to read. *Field of Daisies* offers hope for the future to children of families who suffer generational Alzheimer's. *An Island Just for Us* is a romantic adventure story that takes place in Maine's beautiful and challenging Penobscot Bay. It is all about family and how they meet their problems. A subplot summarizes the social research findings on the effect of our over sexualized culture on young boys. She is presently writing a sequel.

"The kids and I just read the book aloud and loved it!!! It is absolutely wonderful! I read a lot of books and think this is definitely a book to be enjoyed by many readers young and old! I already knew you were talented."

Emily Casto

www.ingramcontent.com/pod-product-compliance
Lightning Source LLC
Chambersburg PA
CBHW041005170626
46815CB00002B/176